CAMP
AUGUSTA

Four Friends Find Fun

Illustrated by Timothy Zulewski.

ISBN: 0-9741760-1-X

Co-published: RS Colmer, EKLEKTIKA Press: 0-9651672-4-0
LCCN: 2004092902

10 9 8 7 6 5 4 3 2   First Printing 2004
Printed in China.

Visit www.personalityinsights.com
www.fourfriends.org

Four Friends Find Fun

Go on an adventure with Derek, Izzy, Sofia and Carl,
as they learn about each other!

Written by V. L. Doyle and Dr. Robert A. Rohm

Illustrated by Timothy Zulewski

Published by Personality Insights, Inc.
Atlanta, GA

Once upon a time, deep in the forest, there was a wonderful campground called Camp Augusta. It was the best place in the entire world. It was FULL of fun!

Four little friends named Derek, Izzy, Sofia and Carl,
all arrived at camp on the same day.

Dynamic Derek was determined to be the first one to start the summer fun. He wanted to set the pace for all of the activities at camp.

Inspiring Izzy could not stop talking about how excited she was!
She had been dreaming of this day since last summer.

Sweet Sofia made treats for all of her friends.
She liked to make everyone feel special.

Cautious Carl wanted to have the perfect campsite —
orderly, neat and clean. He even set up his telescope
for studying the stars later that night.

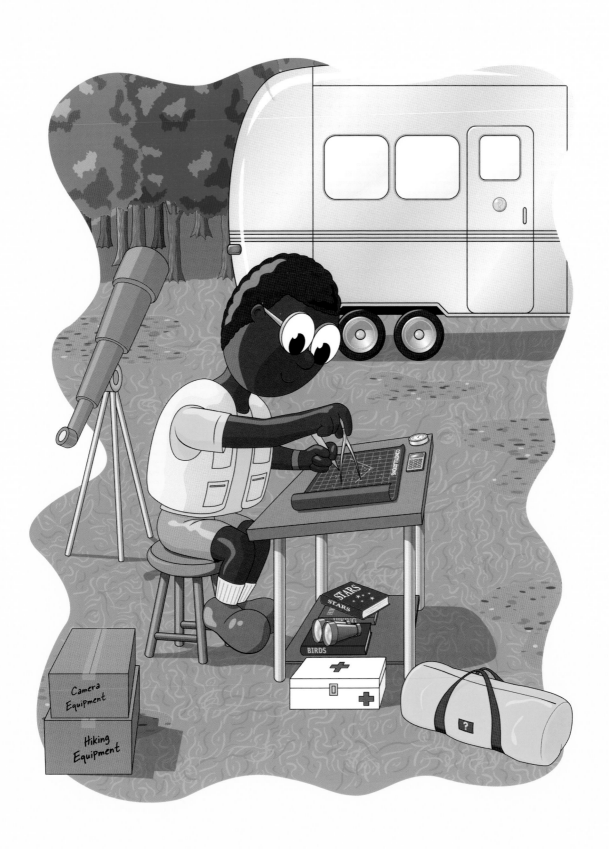

That night the four friends sat around the campfire telling scary stories.

Izzy was a natural born storyteller.
"You know," said Izzy, "I heard that
Princess Augusta still roams around
the Raisin River looking for her lost treasure."

Derek noticed that it was getting late.
He ordered everyone to go to bed and get a good night's sleep.
Tomorrow they were going on a big adventure!

The next morning, the four friends met at the boat dock.
They were going fishing!

Derek was the captain of the boat. He liked to be in charge;
and he was a quick decision maker.

"This is going to be the best fishing trip ever!," exclaimed Izzy.
"I brought special worms for everyone.
The fish will go wild over these!"

Sofia wanted everyone to be safe.
She liked to know what to expect ahead of time.
She was feeling a little fearful about the adventure.

Carl was very organized. He reviewed his checklist
one more time and then gave everyone a life preserver.
He liked to be prepared.

They floated down the river. Derek ordered everyone to row together.
Izzy sang so loud that she scared the fish!
Sofia wanted to be helpful and made sure that nothing
fell out of the boat. Carl studied the map.

"I think I caught a whopper!,"
Izzy squealed with delight.

Right away Derek took over.
"I'm going to reel it in," he informed everyone.

Carl shouted, "Oh no! We are headed for a waterfall."
Sofia felt some raindrops coming down and started to worry.

Derek reeled in their catch.
It was so heavy. What could it be?

It was a treasure chest!

Derek tried his best to open the chest. Izzy marveled at
the sparkles and imagined all of the wonderful things
they would find inside. Sofia did not know what to expect next.
Carl was the first to see the waterfall.

The kids screamed as their boat went over the waterfall and flipped upside down. The treasure chest was lost. They swam to shore and ran to their campsites to get out of the storm.

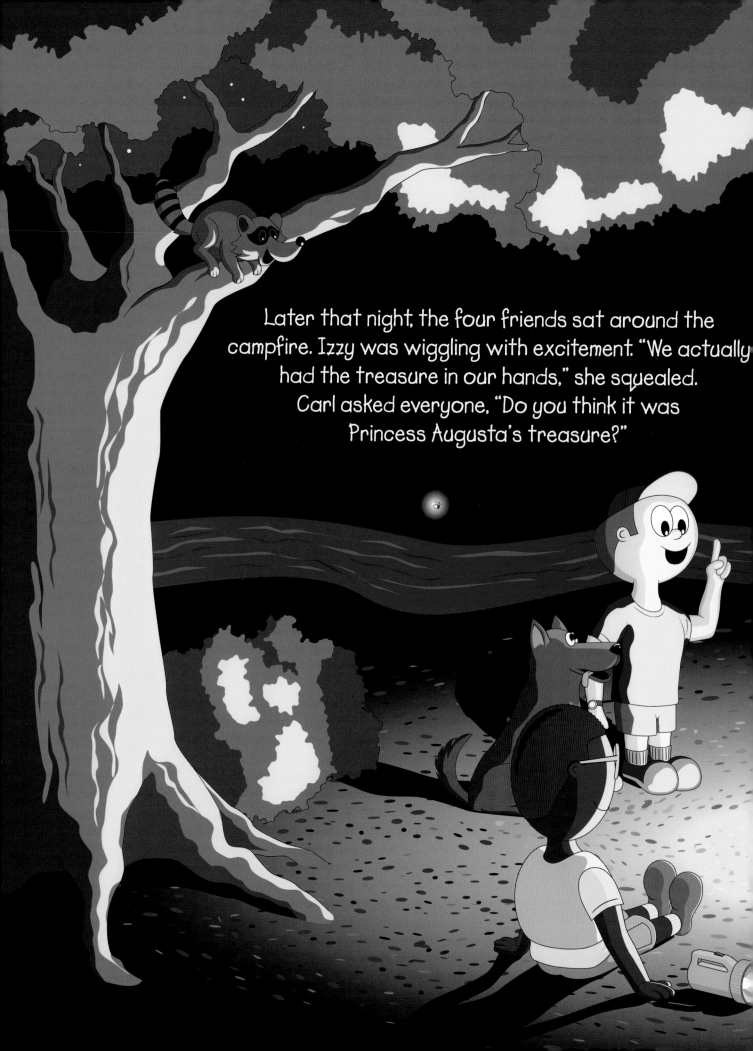

Later that night, the four friends sat around the campfire. Izzy was wiggling with excitement. "We actually had the treasure in our hands," she squealed. Carl asked everyone, "Do you think it was Princess Augusta's treasure?"

"Of course it was, and we are going back out tomorrow
to get it," declared Derek. Izzy bubbled over with excitement.
Carl knew just where to find the treasure chest.
He remembered seeing a willow tree close to where it sank.
Sofia whispered, "Maybe we will need some more help."

Izzy giggled and said, "We are having so much fun!
I KNOW that we will find the treasure chest tomorrow!
We are a great team. By working together
we have all the help we need."

Derek

Derek was a dynamic individual who made decisions easily. He was demanding at times and somewhat controlling in his attitude. He often had more confidence than ability.

Izzy

Izzy was inspiring and full of energy. Her exciting nature made every event adventuresome and fun. She was the life of the party. Sometimes when she was over-excited, she had a tendency to get into trouble.

Sofia

Sofia was sweet and caring. She liked a safe environment in order to stay calm. Although shy at times, she was very thoughtful and considerate of her friends. Sofia had a hard time speaking up when she felt fearful.

Carl

Carl was cautious and careful in all he did. He spent time gathering details in order to create a factual plan. His inquisitive and questioning nature helped ensure safety for his friends. Sometimes Carl's concentration on the task at hand caused him to overlook the value found in close relationships.

Personality Insights, Inc.

Please point out to your child the fact that each of the four friends had different strengths and weaknesses.

Please keep in mind that we are not trying to "stereotype" anyone. We would be the first to promote the fact that everyone is a blend of all four DISC types. No one is purely a D, I, S or C type. We all have some qualities of each of the four styles. Personality types cross all kinds of personal differences (male/female, birth order, race, religion, nationality, etc.).

It is our intent to help children better understand themselves… as well as other children.

For a more in-depth understanding of personality styles visit:
www.personalityinsights.com
or contact us at:

Personality Insights
PO Box 28592
Atlanta, GA 30358
1-800-509-DISC

www.fourfriends.org